CAT TALK

CAT TALK

Patricia MacLachlan *and*
Emily MacLachlan Charest

Illustrated by Barry Moser

KATHERINE TEGEN BOOKS
An Imprint of HarperCollins Publishers

Katherine Tegen Books is an imprint of HarperCollins Publishers.

Cat Talk

Text copyright © 2013 by Patricia MacLachlan and Emily MacLachlan Charest
Illustrations copyright © 2013 by Barry Moser.
All rights reserved. Manufactured in China.

Library of Congress Cataloging-in-Publication Data is available.
ISBN 978-0-06-027978-3 (trade bdg.) —ISBN 978-0-06-027979-0 (lib. bdg.)

Typography by Dana Fritts
13 14 15 16 17   SCP   10 9 8 7 6 5 4 3 2 1
❖
First Edition

For Lesléa and Mary
  and their Princess Sheba Darling,
  and in memory of Sammy.
    Love,
      P.M. and E.C.

For B.C. and Kristin, two of my favorite felinophiles.
      —B.M.

Tough Tom

You opened the window
And I walked in.
I didn't want to
But it was cold outside
And dark.
And I was hungry.

You opened the window
And I walked in
With a torn ear
And a scratch on my nose.
It was warm
And you had food
And a blanket.

At first I was scared.
I was used to rooftops
And rain
And snow
And dark.
And fighting with other cats.

But you opened the window
And I walked in.

Lily

I was born in the big red barn
With cows
And horses
And one gray donkey named
Rose.
There is sweet-smelling hay,
And the breathing of cows,
And horse snorts.
I have a best friend.
Don't tell—
Please!
I wouldn't want anyone to know this.
But

I think he's a mouse.

Tuck

Under the blankets
Is the best place—
Except for cozy drawers
And the mitten box
And any dirty laundry.
Every morning I sneak under the covers
While they're sleeping

Dark

Warm

Quiet

And find a nice ankle to lick with my rough
    wrinkled tongue.

Look.

He's still sleeping.

He'll be surprised.

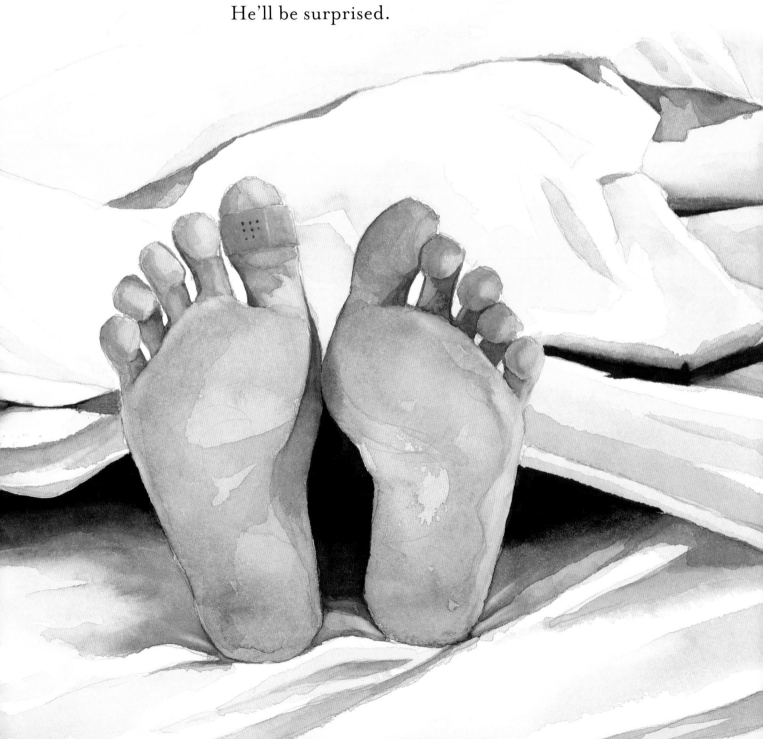

Princess Sheba Darling

I love me.
I have a beautiful face.
I have a beautiful coat.
And a beautiful fan tail.
I spread it out
Like a peacock
To show people how special I am.
As hard as I try, I could never be more beautiful
Than I am
Now.

Alice

Wait!
I hear water running.
I love bath time!
When you're in the bath, I sit on the edge and watch.
I lean way over and sip the nice warm water.
Bubbles fly
And drift
And pop in the air
Like whispers.
I don't care.
I like the taste of soap.

Minnie

You can't see me when it's dark.
My fur is the color of night.
I am a shadow,
   Hiding next to the black walnut tree
   Slipping around the old lilac
   Walking the fence.
Maybe you think I am
   The tree
   The lilac
   The fence.
You don't see me.

But if you look very closely,
You can see
My
   Big
   Bright
   Yellow
   Eyes.

Henry

She got married
In the garden
In a long white dress
With flowers in her hair.

Cats don't get married, you know.
But I watched
Hidden
Next to a wild aster.

I don't care for weddings,
But I like her.
And I love that long white dress.
I slept on it
All night long
I slept
As the white silk gathered like a cloud
Around me.

I love the girl.
I love that long white dress.

Bett

Here are my three kittens.
Soon someone will name them.
  Tangerine, maybe
  Midnight
  Splash

If it were up to me, their names would be
SLEEPY
She is orange and good.
NOISY
He is black-and-white and meows.
  Hush, hush.
TROUBLE
She is many colors.
She digs in the dirt of the potted plant.
She eats the violet blooms
And climbs up the curtains.
Sometimes she goes to the bathroom
On the
Old
Red
Persian
Rug.
So far no one has noticed.

Sylvie, the Boss

I am the boss cat.
I twitch my tail to prove it.
I boss the dogs.
I boss my people.
I boss Romeo, the cat I live with,
 Whenever I can.
I like three things:
My food
My windowsill
My people.
And that's enough.

Romeo

I am a lover cat.
I love everyone.
I fall over onto people I love.
You can pet me anytime
Anywhere.
You can wake me and I'll play.
I fall over onto Sylvie, too.
She hisses, but I still love her.
I love everyone.

Peony

I am a flower.
My face blooms
Big
Fluffy
Full.
Under all this fur
You can hardly see my eyes
  Blue.
You can hardly see my nose
  Pink.
They brush me to keep out tangles and ticks.
What no one knows
Is that under my big coat
I am
Little.

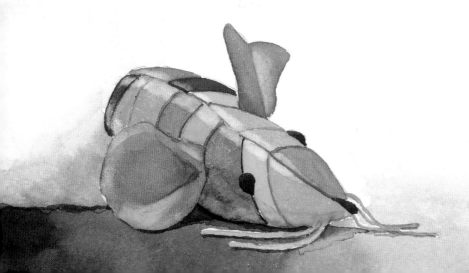

Simon

I play hide-and-seek all the time.
I hide.
I leap—
  Sometimes people scream!
I bat—
  They run!
I chase—
  They stand on chairs.
I pounce—
  They put me in the pantry and close the door.
Scaredy-cats!

All the Voices of Eddie

I have a job.
I greet people at the office door.
I sleep on the copy machine.
I run to the phone when it rings.

I have many voices.
I chirp when people come in.
Chrrrp—hello.
Meow—a snack please, please??
Hiss!—go away.
Yowl!—something is wrong! A mouse in the house!
Chatter, chatter—a bird at the window.
Purr—I like you.

All these voices are different
But all these voices are me.

And then
When I want to
I make no sound at all.
I close my eyes
And
  Silently
  Quietly
Pretend you're not there at all for me to talk to.

Goodbye.

The illustrations for *Cat Talk* were executed in transparent watercolor on paper hand made at the Hayle Mill in Kent, England, for the Royal Watercolour Society. The book was designed by Barry Moser and Dana Fritts. The typeface used is Mrs Eaves, which was designed by Zuzana Licko in 1996. It is named after Sarah Eaves, wife of printer John Baskerville. The display faces used are Federlyn NF, Hadriano Light, and Wade Sans Light. The book is printed on 128gsm Chinese Gold East Matt Art, made by the Shan Dong Sun Paper Industry Joint Stock Co. Ltd. of Yanzhou City, China. It was printed by South China Printing Co. Ltd. in Hong Kong.